DELICIOUS AGE GAP

First Time MM Older Man Story

Michael Levi

ISBN: 9798777289728
Imprint: Independently published

2nd edition

Cover design by: Michael Levi

CONTENTS

Title Page

Copyright

Chapter 1 — 1

Chapter 2 — 3

Chapter 3 — 8

Chapter 4 — 11

Chapter 5A — 13

Chapter 5B — 19

Straight to Gay Series and More — 25

About the Author — 27

CHAPTER 1

I lived with a handsome, overconfident, 18 years old guy. He had a man cave where he watched movies and played video games. Being the guy he was, he always brought his friends over, and they were just as lust-inducing as he was. They threw parties there and made a lot of noise, but it didn't bother me.

There was something he didn't know about me. A tiny little secret I kept to myself – I loved watching them dicking around in his man cave.

I knew I was doing something wrong, but I couldn't stop. Trying to make me feel better about it, I always told myself that I was just ogling them and not him. And that was how it always was. I drooled over them and seldom paid any attention to him. They were all so young, energetic, and *big*. And more often than not, they hung out with just their briefs on – and they looked absolutely delicious that way.

His man cave had a bathroom with a hole only I knew about. There was a hidden corridor that I used to make my way to the other side of said hole, and that was how I spied on them partying.

I loved drooling over the shape of their bulges. They looked so plump and big. They were 18, but they already looked much older than their age. They were manly, had athletic bodies, and their voices were thick and heavy.

I was bisexual and my wife didn't know anything about that. I'd never had sex with a man, my sexual urges crashing through the roof of my mind every day. I thought about that all the time and it was making me lose my mind about it. I needed a gay fuck so bad!

One of the best things about his man cave was watching them take a leak. That's where I always got a spectacular view of their oversized shafts, and also the best angles.

My mouth salivated every time they pulled down their underwear and unloaded their pee into the toilet. *Ah, if only that hole could turn into a glory hole.* If only I dared to invite them to try my mouth…

Keeping up appearances and not cheating on my wife were more important than being selfish… right? I wasn't planning anything, but now I was already feeling curious.

What if I dared them to do it?

CHAPTER 2

The guy I lived with was getting into his car and was going back to college. He'd invited his friends over, and I knew they were going to throw another party there.

It was another opportunity for me to savor their big bulges, so I walked down where the hole was and began to ogle them.

As usual, they had no pants on and their bulges looked plump and heavy. They were all sitting on the couches, legs wide open, and drinking as much juice as they could.

I asked myself — could I really trick those young men into putting their manhoods inside the hole? They should be more willing to do that after a few rounds, I concluded. Not that they were going to be drunk or anything like that. Just more *willing*.

I scurried away upstairs, grabbed a pen and paper to write the following: "Free Cocksucking". Then, I went back behind the hole and put the note there.

"I'm going to take a leak, guys. Back in a bit," one of the studs said. Good! I thought. He was going to be the first to see the note.

As he stumbled in, I noticed how fast my heart was beating. This was my chance to suck him off, and nothing was going to stop me now. I could just imagine his hard, enraged dick drilling into my mouth.

His name was Max and when he slid down his underwear, I was able to check on his huge manhood up close. It was about five inches soft, cut. Wow! What a view and what a man he was.

He grabbed his cock and aimed it at the toilet. He unloaded his pee for a good minute until he was empty. Damn, the bladder that man had.

He was shaking his cock. I was dripping pre-cum like a faucet. My mouth was watering as I smelled his musky cock and manliness.

Just like his other friends, Max had a toned body. They all went to the gym often, played football, were taller than me by a head, and looked older than their age.

In contrast, I was a puny, fragile man in my forties. If you put me in between those big men and took a photo of the scene, it would probably make a good cover for some erotica books!

Since he had just his briefs on, I was able to check on the curves of his legs. His feet were enormous and sported a good amount of very noticeable veins too.

I had a fetish for manly feet, and I couldn't take my eyes off them.

Max had forgotten to turn on the light in the cubicle. When he noticed how dark the place was, he decided to do that. It was then he saw the note above the hole in the wall.

"Free Cocksucking, huh?" He asked, and my cock grew by an inch. I could barely contain myself from jacking off right then and there, but I wanted to focus on what the young man was going to do.

Just as I suspected, Max was way more willing this time. He stumbled toward the hole, his ball sack and shaft growing and filling my vision.

What a privileged view I had!

The hole was big enough for his incredible rod, and I was drooling from both sides of my mouth. I thought I was going to faint.

The heat coming from the jovial man was almost palpable. Right now, the only thing I could do was to open my hungry mouth and allow his big bulge to come in.

Max turned off the light and the room fell into darkness again. He was still himself, and knowing that was making this all the better.

The only noise I could hear was coming from his friends, but they felt so distant. I could hear the young man breathing heavily. He didn't say a word, and neither did I.

Obediently, I let his big manhood slip between my moist lips and I held it in my mouth the same way a dog holds a bone. Slowly, very slowly, I started to mouth the 18-year-old's manly bulge. I was trying, without knowing, not to let him figure out who was behind the glory hole. His dick got bigger and stonier as I began to nurse on his big manhood.

I was drooling and couldn't wrap my head around what was happening. At last, I was holding that gigantic manhood in my hungry mouth. I knew he was horny as hell. It had probably been some time since someone serviced his big cock like that. He craved this blowjob, and I was happy I was doing it for him.

I knew he wanted me to take it slow. I noticed he wanted to be cocksucked slowly and to make it last as long as possible. I could feel his dick getting bigger inside my mouth, holding it between my lips like the slut I was. I continued mouthing on it, sucking his big member until it was fully wet and pulsating. Out of nowhere, I heard Max letting out a long, cracked moan as his cock began to ooze white cream. He was squirting it out, and it was hot and creamy. It kept on unloading nice and slow while I sucked his dirty man tool and mopped his warm manly juice. I was overflowing with joy.

There I was sucking this alpha, young man's big cock through a hole in the wall for the first time. I was so glad he fell for my trap. I gave his shaft a little squeeze, and then he eased it out. He didn't say anything and just left the cubicle.

I stayed where I was, my cock hard as a rock. I was waiting to see if someone else was going to come to use the restroom. I was not disappointed when I noticed Gary coming in.

He was a little out of it but could still process everything going on around him – and that made me feel less guilty. With care, he slid down his briefs, pulled his dick out, and started to pee like his bladder was infinite. I was drooling over what I was seeing, and I wasn't going to hide that.

He was a bit taller than Max, his cock slightly thicker, uncut, and was wearing blue briefs.

Once he was done taking a leak, he stood in front of me shaking his member and showing it off to my glistening eyes. I felt as if he wanted to tease me, even though I knew Max had not told anyone about the hole and that Gary hadn't seen the note yet.

He turned the light on and had the same reaction as Max did. He guided his soft, uncut cock into the hole, and I stood where I was, admiring it. I was drooling uncontrollably and making plans on how I was going to suckle it.

I knew he wanted me to take it slow, as I did with Max, so I was very careful with his man tool. Quietly, I put the soft cock into my waiting mouth.

Slowly, he helped me guide his huge package in between my naughty lips. With overflowing excitement and care, I closed my lips around the 18-year-old's manly dick and laid it in my mouth like the whore I was. I could feel his veiny cock getting bigger.

His cock was throbbing and emanating a manly smell that almost made me lose my mind.

Just as with Max, I sucked on Gary's gigantic shaft and felt lucky I could do this. I felt special as I finally had someone — or better, two young men — who appreciated my cocksucking skills.

When he was done, he turned off the light and walked out of the cubicle without saying a word. I decided I should not push my luck further and removed the note from the hole.

Then, I covered it however I could and walked upstairs.

I greeted the guys as they left the house and went to my bedroom. It was time to fantasize about those athletic and manly bodies after the successful experiment I had.

I flopped down on the bed and began to stroke my hard cock. It wasn't hard to get me going, so in under two minutes, my dick began to throb. I decorated my t-shirt with my hot cum.

I let out a deep and long moan as I cherished the events that had just happened. I was certainly going to try again the following day, and my next objective was to suck off the other guys.

They were going to come home tomorrow, and I wanted them to know that there was someone who could take care of their big, manly bulges any time they wanted to pee.

I cleaned myself up and headed back to the basement. I grabbed some cushion and put it in the hole to make it more comfortable for the guys.

They were going to love my attention to detail.

CHAPTER 3

I kissed my wife, wished her good luck, and went downstairs to spy on the guys when they were back. I had my note in my hand and put it back where it was yesterday.

The guys kicked off things early today. It wasn't even 9 AM, and they were already partying. Their muscles flexed. My eyes cherished their manly bodies. They were enjoying their drinks and watching college football.

Before long, Jimmy came into the cubicle to take a leak and also forgot to turn on the light.

He was a bit shorter than the two I serviced yesterday, but I noticed that his cock was longer and thicker.

Just like Gary, Jimmy was also pissing a huge load. As soon as he finished and turned on the light, he had a different reaction from the guys yesterday. He didn't look surprised and put one of his fingers inside the hole.

Maybe he figured out something was up given how long his friends were taking to unload their piss?

He was standing in front of me, holding his soft dick.

I was so horny that I dared to show my mouth in the hole to make him see my malicious tongue flicking. I figured he was feeling horny as fuck as well and, thus, I wasn't surprised when I saw his big bulge coming in my direction. My mouth was ready and waiting to service the 18-year-old's huge cock.

Jimmy had a thick hairy bush. I made sure not to scare him off as I wrapped my lips around his beautiful dick. I started to mouth his cock, relishing its taste. His dick was getting harder and harder while I sucked his enormous instrument. I noticed how much he loved my cocksucking.

He started to moan and groan loudly. In a matter of minutes, he was releasing all his hot milk into my hungry mouth. Making sure that nothing spilled out, I cleaned him from his cockhead to his balls. He was delicious.

Jimmy put his cock back into his underwear and gave a nod of approval as he left the cubicle.

Crap! He figured out what was going on, I thought. Still, did he know it was the 'funny husband' doing this?

Moments later, it was Wellington's turn. Big Welly was about to get the blowjob of his life, and I was going to swallow every drop of his hot, creamy milk.

He had no shirt on, and I drooled over his flawless body. He came in through the door looking more aware of his surroundings than the other guys, and it was then I knew they were all going to find out that a glory hole was in the bathroom.

Welly's bulge was huger than all the others were. I licked my lips and drooled as I imagined having his manhood in my hungry mouth.

Welly pulled his underwear down to take a piss and I treasured every curve and vein on his oversized man tool. His bush was as dense as the Amazon rainforest and I noticed how proud he was of his cock. The way he was holding it was very telling of that.

He pissed into the toilet like a horse and then shook his instrument until his cock was fully clean. He held it there and admired his own manhood for a couple of seconds until he turned right and spotted the note.

Just like last time, I put my tongue outside the hole and flipped it up and down naughtily. I figured that if the young man didn't want to be sucked off, he would just walk away.

The young stud was staring at the hole, and his bulge was growing. He pulled down his briefs and I noticed that his cock was a thing of beauty.

It appeared to be the longest cock in his group of friends. It was easily at least 8 inches hard and looked thick as fuck.

"Looks like he wasn't shitting me," he growled, and an evil smile showed up on his face.

He guided his rock-hard tool into my hungry mouth. I began to suck it hungrily and greedily.

I wondered if the other guys were hearing this, but did it even matter? They all probably already knew about the glory hole. They just didn't know and care that it was the husband servicing their young cocks.

Welly was loving how much I was taking care of him and, suddenly, I felt his cock throbbing like a pipe under high pressure. Seconds later, he was unloading his warm, generous load of cream into my mouth. It was so sweet and salty at the same time. He was feeding me properly.

Just like with the other guys, I made sure his cock was squeaky-clean and that I didn't lose a drop of his warm milk.

He walked out of the cabin, and his friends queried if he liked the glory hole. They really all knew about it, and I wasn't surprised by that at all.

That morning went by perfectly. The hunks were having a good time in their man cave. They looked happy to be there. The glory hole was a good boost for their morale.

At some point, I heard Gary saying he liked the cubicle and wouldn't mind having one at his home. I was overjoyed to hear that and decided I was going to keep inviting them to come here.

Their party stopped in the evening and I invited them to come home tomorrow. I was going to make them happy again.

CHAPTER 4

So, I decided I wanted to mix things up a bit. Other than the dinner I'd promised to the studs, I desired to service them in another way and to make them even happier for being in my house.

They were going to throw a party at the swimming pool and that was the perfect opportunity for me to suck their dicks more spectacularly.

The house had a swimming pool. I could go there and make four glory holes, one for each of them.

I could turn the party into a marathon of cocksucking with just one rule: a limit of 30 seconds of continuous cocksucking until they all fed me their creamy loads.

They would have to compete among themselves to find out who could last my naughty lips the longest. I was pretty sure that my crushes were going to find that thrilling.

The advantage of that plan was the maintenance of my secrecy. They weren't going to know that I was the one manning the glory holes. The downside was that I was going to be limited to blowjobs yet again.

I could tell them that they were always welcome for a blowjob if they promised to keep their mouth shut about it. Since they all seemed happy to have their delicious cocks serviced, I had a good chance of making that plan work.

So, that meant I had two options:

1. To give them the blowjob of their lives (Chapter 5A)

2. Let them all share me in my bed and do whatever they wanted (Chapter 5B)

CHAPTER 5A

Just after my wife left to go to her office, I headed to the bathroom by the swimming pool and made four big glory holes in the wall. I added a bit of cushion on the sides to keep their cocks comfortable.

I set up the timer on my phone to keep track of the time.

The holes were wide enough for their hairy sacks. I was going to have a feast with their thick bushes.

They came in the morning with nothing but their sexy boxer briefs on and headed for the swimming pool. They started making some barbecue and the smell of cooked meat quickly impregnated the air.

They drank a little more juice and chatted loudly. Eventually, one of them headed towards the bathroom to pee.

It was Max, the first guy I serviced in the glory hole in their man cave. I had left another note, and this time it was in the bathroom itself.

It said, "Free Cocksucking, but only if everyone comes over. And the reward is some candies for whoever lasts the longest."

Naughty as he was, all he could do was to say, "Okay."

He headed out, and I heard him raising his voice when he said, "Hey guys, come see this."

They all came to the bathroom and some could barely stand on their two feet, as usual. Some were also wet after being in the swimming pool.

I hopped from hole to hole, eager to ogle at the guys striding in. The bathroom had golden mood lights, highlighting the perfection of their bodies.

Strong legs, confident postures, wide torsos, six-packs, and generous bulges — they had everything I wanted. My mouth was drooling as I waited for them to take the bait.

They all looked at each other maliciously and pulled down their boxer briefs at the same time. Oh, what a sight for sore eyes!

Their cocks grew bigger and thicker as they anticipated the divine cocksucking they were going to get. Their balls seemed to glow under the golden light of the bathroom.

They grabbed their big cocks confidently with their huge hands and guided their instruments to their respective glory holes.

From left to right, they were positioned as follows: Max, Jimmy, Welly, and Gary. Patiently, their cocks came in. My rock-hard dick was oozing pre-cum, and my new underwear was getting stained by my uncontrollable leak.

I positioned myself in front of Max's big cock and, slowly, wrapped my lips around his purple mushroom head. He emitted a loud and long moan as I began to mouth his appetizing dick.

My nose and eyes were buried in his thick bush. I couldn't see and breathe like normal, but I could feel how warm he was.

I used my hand to massage his balls and kept on sucking the full length of his shaft. I was so glad I was sucking on his big man tool.

Before long, the timer beeped, and I moved to the next hunk: Jimmy.

Kicking the wall so that I worshiped his big slab of meat right away, I remembered why he was one of my favorites. Muscles on top of muscles, curves perfectly defined, tanned skin, and a cock-head much bigger than any I'd seen.

I buried my face deep into his thick manly bush and wrapped my hungry mouth around his gigantic tool. His masculine maleness felt fantastic in my warm mouth.

Gradually, I sucked his rock-hard cock ever so slowly. I relished and savored it to make sure I was pleasing the big man in front of me. I wanted him to get all the respect he deserved.

I began to nurse him like a greedy doggie. He moaned and groaned increasingly more. Suddenly, the stud said with a low, hoarse voice, "Suck my big, young cock off, bitch."

I got another beep from the timer and moved to the next guy: Welly.

He was a bit more patient than Jimmy. I buried my face once again and my mouth loved his shaft. He emitted a long and raspy moan when I wrapped my lips around his big cockhead.

My heart pounding, I sucked on his enormous shaft. It was mine only right now.

I took my time as I milked his delicious manhood. I savored his sturdy, hard dong respectfully and showed him what a great cocksucker I was.

Then, I heard him saying, "Suck on it and show me how much you love it."

I sure showed him that. He was moaning, looking closer to his climax than the guys before him.

It was now the next guy's turn. Gary looked impatient, just like Jimmy. He shook his cock and urged me to hurry up.

I moved to be in front of his big man tool and licked my lips as I anticipated the feeling of having another young cock in my mouth. Thirty seconds were enough to get him in the mood without boring out his friends.

I opened my willing, warm mouth. Differently than when we did with the other hunks, I encouraged Gary to be more proactive. He moved in closer to the hole and plunged his big man tool in it.

I latched on his delicious dick and began to suck it. I venerated his manly shaft and didn't feel ashamed. He was leaking pre-cum like a broken faucet.

Gary was moaning hard as a rock. To my surprise, he was getting hornier and hornier at a faster rate than the other guys were. I felt his big cock throbbing like a pipe under high pressure. He was feeding me his hot milk before I could even mumble anything.

I made sure I swallowed all of his very generous load and that he was well cleaned before I moved back to the first guy.

His friends cracked jokes and laughed that he blew his load too quickly. They hinted that he should stop jacking off too often, or that else he would drop the ball when fucking a woman for real.

I giggled at the jokes that they made. Gary left the bathroom shouting obscene words to his friends.

I savored the first man's cock again, then the second and the third. I mouthed their wet skins and sucked their delicious pre-cum. They were all feeling so horny and infatuated by my hungry mouth.

I made sure I showed their shafts the respect they deserved. I always started with their mushroom heads and caressed their oversized balls with all the care I could muster.

My cock was as big and hard as it could get. I pulled down my briefs and jerked off.

I lost track of time and could only hear the beeps from the timer before I moved to the next guy. I was in a complete state of ecstasy and could only think of sucking the delicious cocks in front of me.

My crushes were all loving the service they were getting. Their groans were so loud the neighbors had to be hearing everything.

It was a good ad to pique their curiosity and make them try the glory holes in the bathroom as well.

"Suck on my big cock nice and slow."

"Yes, keep going, bitch. I want to feed you my cum and make sure you understand who the boss is in this house."

These were all common phrases I heard during the marathon. Reaching their orgasms, I noticed that their dicks were already throbbing.

The next to blow his load into my hungry mouth was Welly. He squirted his load out, a huge smile appearing on his face.

I made sure to get every drop of his hot, creamy man milk and clean him up. I kissed his big mushroom head before he left the bathroom, a grin on his young face.

Then came Jimmy's turn, and he fed me a very generous load of juicy man milk as well. I grabbed his balls and pleaded for him to give me everything he had.

He didn't disappoint me. His hot man balls pulsated in my

hands and his cock stiffened as he kept delivering his salty cream in my wet mouth.

I sucked his shaft and, especially, the top of his mushroom head to make sure he was well taken care of. I also kissed his delicious cock and then slapped it to tell the young man I was done.

He sported a grin on his face as he left the bathroom, and Max was smiling, knowing he won their contest.

I put his juicy, big man cock into my mouth another time and sucked it. I made sure I took it slowly before I gradually increased the pace.

Max was eating the hole raw, and my face kept hitting against his groin. I put my hands on the wall to support my weight and felt my cock throbbing.

Max was at his climax. I felt his big man dick pulsating as well. We unloaded our man milk together, and I savored his generous load. My cum came in short bursts as my cock stiffened and flicked in all directions.

He was moaning and it was turning me even more than I already was. Max mumbled, "Keep sucking me off like that, bitch. You know how to suck cocks."

And I sure obeyed the confident, young man in front of me. He let out a long moan as he unloaded his last burst of cum. I cleaned his shaft thoroughly to make sure I didn't waste a drop of his delicious man juice.

Before he left, I grabbed the box of candy I had brought and handed it to him. Max said, "Thanks, cocksucker. Keep this up, and I'm certainly coming back here often. I need my big dick sucked and taken care of. Love getting a blowjob whenever I want."

He left with a wide smile on his face. I sat on the floor. That marathon sure consumed most of my energy reserves.

I closed my eyes and began to dream wild, naughty fantasies involving those hot young men. My hand found my semi-hard cock and I began to stroke it gently.

My other hand found my hairy hole and I began to moan as I masturbated myself.

Surprisingly, I still felt I could cream another time. I kept jacking off until I felt my climax exploding.

I unloaded my creamy man milk all over myself and took deep breaths as I began to relax. I was skilled at sucking off dicks, and I was proud of that.

Now, all those young men had even more reasons to keep coming back. I couldn't wait until I could have their juicy man meats between my hungry lips another time.

CHAPTER 5B

The young studs came back, scurried off to the pool with grins on their faces, and kicked off their party. They started making some barbecue and I wished I could join them and have a nice cooked meal as well.

I had, however, more important things to do. I couldn't just reveal myself to them bluntly during the barbecue, so I decided that a more imaginative approach was going to be better.

I headed to the bedroom and made a nice and comfy glory hole for the guys in a fake wall. Then, I put some notes in the house and backyard to guide them to my bedroom.

I wanted them to take the bait, thinking that they were going to get just another juicy blowjob. I needed to make them feel safe and at home before I offered my sweet body to them.

Once I was done putting the last note, I headed back to my bedroom and hid behind the glory hole.

Tapping my foot on the floor, I waited until one of the young studs scurried back into the room.

I heard the door opening. It was Max, who was eager to ask, "Mr. Robert, is this you again?"

He looked all tanned and delicious. I wish I could devour him right then and there. His beardless face still had a hint of his innocence, but I could see that it was quickly fading. His muscles flexed with each step he took, mesmerizing me.

Then, he noticed the note and the glory hole just below it. He grinned menacingly and slid down his wet boxer briefs. He had recently been in the swimming pool playing with the other guys, I guessed.

His cock was already getting harder and swelling in front of his thick, dark bush.

"Hmm, I knew something was up," he said as he neared the hole. My mouth was already drooling.

His big cock was a sight to behold. Long, very thick, easily 8 inches hard. Damn, what a piece of meat that guy had. He was so lucky to have been born like that.

He put his cock inside the glory hole slowly and carefully. My waiting mouth wrapped itself around the skin of his mushroom head and I began to suck him nice and slow.

He began to moan and groan loudly. When he was completely under my control, his eyes shut and his mouth drooling, I decided to show myself.

I brought the wall down with minimal effort, and Max was oblivious to me.

With the weight of my body, I pushed him down, and he fell on his ass. It was only then that he noticed what I was doing.

My hungry mouth was still all over his juicy man tool, his legs wide open. I could see the hair on the underside of his hip and between his smooth asscheeks and my free hand went for it.

"What..." He mumbled, shutting his eyes. He didn't comment on the fact that I was sucking him off.

I resumed what I was doing, worshiping his dick. I caressed his big feet, strong legs and massaged his nicely defined abs. His body was so delicious!

"Max!" I heard the other studs dropping in. They all seemed surprised and excited at the same time. They looked at me, Max, and themselves.

"So, it's just as we thought," Jimmy said as he grinned evilly.

Arousal replaced their shock. They all looked horny and hungry for my big cocksucking mouth. I was happy to know that they desired me.

They all pulled down their wet boxer briefs to the floor and Jimmy positioned himself behind me. He made me sit on my knees and guide my hole towards his rock-hard cock.

He put his hand on my back and penetrated me carefully. His cock was huge, and I screamed as he pounded in me.

"You like a big cock up your ass, eh, Mr. Robert?" Jimmy said with a mocking laugh.

Wellington and Gary didn't want to feel left out, so they started to kiss and hug each other. Their kisses looked passionate and their hands danced around their perfect bodies.

Max couldn't wrap his head around what was happening. His eyes were shut, his mouth drooling like a waterfall, and his shaft was getting warmer and warmer. I knew that he was overjoyed by my cocksucking.

I kept sucking on his shaft as he said, "Keep sucking me off like this, and you might just get a nice surprise."

I obeyed him without a problem. His cock was just so juicy and wet at that point I had no difficulty going up and down on it. Damn, what a man-meat he had!

I felt his cock throbbing as if it was about to explode, and then he shot his hot creamy man milk inside my mouth. It came in short bursts and the volume was enough to fill my whole mouth.

He was young and had a very generous load. I imagined he could still go for a second round if he wanted to. Guys his age were always pumped up!

I swallowed all the milk he fed me and made sure his rock-hard cock was clean before I eased it out of my mouth.

He laid his back on the floor and took a deep, long breath as he started to relax. His eyes were still closed, and he had a nice grin on his face. He truly approved of my handiwork on his big cock.

Big Welly noticed I had a free hole and knelt in front of me. I faced his enormous, rock-hard cock and kissed it. It was a kiss of good luck and a promise that I was going to service him, just like I did with Max.

"Suck on it like the bitch you are," he mumbled and then opened a grin.

I wrapped my mouth around his big man tool and started to suckle on it gently. Max's cum still wetted my lips, helping me with sucking off his thick shaft.

Jimmy was still pounding my ass hard and confidently. He often caressed my lower back and asscheeks to help keep me going. I moaned and groaned every time his huge hands moved around the underside of my hips.

Jimmy's hands were so soft. He never had to bust his ass off. His touch was as nice as that of a woman. He knew how to arouse me, and I was happy this virile man was ramming it in and out of me.

Gary wanted to help Jimmy, and he dropped to his knees behind me too. Easing his prick inside my ass, he made me squeal. Two bullies were eating me raw and I was loving every second of it.

I could only scream and groan at the same time. Damn, their cocks were almost too big for me to handle.

"Take it slow, guys. I want to be able to walk after this, okay?"

Gary and Jimmy heard my plea and toned their thrusts down a little. I was happy with that because it meant I was going to be able to focus on Welly's manly tool in front of me.

"He's so tight," Gary mumbled.

"Yeah, he really is. Damn, wish I'd known before that gay sex is this good. Might have tried it before," Jimmy said.

"Me too," Gary agreed and grinned.

They kept pounding my sweet little ass, their balls hitting my asscheeks. Just as with exhausted Max on the floor, my mind had almost completely lost sense of what I was doing and what was happening in front of me.

All I knew was that I wanted to keep mouthing Welly's manly tool in front of me and moan in pleasure by the pounding my ass was getting.

These young guys were so pumped up! It had been already at least 10 minutes and they were still thrusting in my ass non-stop. Their hands were caressing my asscheeks and getting a feeling of it.

Damn, if only I had known that they were so receptive to gay sex, I'd have invited them to my bedroom days ago!

I felt Welly's thick rod throbbing and I knew he was getting close to his climax. His body stiffened, his big sack contracted, and began to unload his very generous load inside my hungry mouth.

He was moaning and I was gulping his hot creamy milk like a street slut. Damn, he had even more in him than Max.

I didn't waste a drop and swallowed all the nectar he fed me. He emitted a long and deep moan and fell on the floor, his lungs breathing hard for air.

The guys still had so much energy to turn, but right now they needed some rest. To remediate that, I told them I had some Monsters in my fridge. They scurried off there and returned in less than a minute.

They hurried downstairs and came back in under a minute. Once again, they looked horny and full of energy. Their cocks stood confidently in front of their hairy sacks.

I flicked my hand and asked them to stand behind me. They looked at each other and grinned. I was going to have two more very thick and long cocks inside of me!

They positioned themselves behind my hurt ass and guided their big man cocks into my hole.

I felt one cock coming in and then the other. A scream escaped my lips, but I got used to their size right away. Their cocks were so juicy and my hole wrapped around their man tools perfectly.

It was my first time doing that. It was our first time, in fact. These guys never had sex with a man before in their lives. From the looks of it, though, I felt that they were going to try what we were doing several more times in the future.

These hunks weren't just having fun with me — they were turning me into their plaything. I looked back and noticed them kissing each other. I was so glad I opened up their thick heads to gay sex.

I watched them making out while I punched the clown. Jimmy was kissing Gary. Welly was kissing Max. Damn, they were really into it.

They kept on pounding in my ass. It hurt, but it was so good I was drooling. I was moaning and groaning louder with each of their thrusts. They had a nice rhythm and nobody was out of sync.

It was easy, once again, to lose awareness of my surroundings. I could feel the pleasure of having four young men inside of me. It was a dream come true.

I felt one of the cocks throbbing and, then, a huge amount of load painted the walls of my tight hole. Seconds later, the next guy was doing the same. Then, the third guy began to fill me with his generous load until the next one replaced him.

I heard long moans coming from them as they finished their good work on my ass. I lied down heavily on the floor, gasping for air. All the guys did the same. I fell asleep quickly and so did they.

I was the first to wake up and hurried them to get up. The sun was already falling behind the buildings, and I knew that my wife was about to come home.

I convinced everyone to keep their mouths shut about what happened. It didn't take me a lot of effort to do that because they all enjoyed gangbanging on my ass and getting a nice blowjob service from me.

I promised more for when they came back, and they all grinned in response. They were so overconfident, and I found it a huge turn-on.

What could I say? I was one damn good cocksucker.

The End

If you want to read the other books in the series, check them out here:

1. Old Friend: A Straight to Gay MM First Time Story
2. My Dear Professor: A Straight to Gay MM First Time Story
3. Up in the Mountain: First Time MM Age Gap Story

And leave a review if you liked the book. It always helps me so much!

STRAIGHT TO GAY SERIES AND MORE

SERIES – EXECUTIVE SUBMISSION

1. Hard in the Office 1: A Straight to Gay MM Story
2. Hard in the Office 2: No Pity for the Miserable Incel
3. Hard in the Office 3: An Incel's Tale of Degrading Humiliation
4. Hard in the Office 4: Bending the Incel Boss
5. Hard in the Office 5: Taming the Incel Spy
6. Hard in the Office 6: Lectured by the Boss

SERIES – OBEY ME

First time gay peppered with age gap.

1. Prep School Obedience 1
2. Prep School Obedience 2
3. Prep School Obedience 3

Other related stories

1. Filthy Wish: A Gay Man of the House on Younger Man Steamy Story
2. Tight and Clenching: A Man of the House on Younger Man Steamy Story
3. Ganged, Used and Devoured: 5 Man of the House and Brat Story Bundle
4. Subdued by the Gay Sitter: Helping the Man of the House
5. Subdued by the Gay Sitter: His Bully's Humiliating Submission

6. Subdued by the Gay Sitter: The Straight Quarterback's First Time

7. Subdued by the Gay Sitter: Straight Jock is put in his Place

8. Used by the Man of the House: 3 OBSCENE Brat Stories

ABOUT THE AUTHOR

Michael Levi's biggest passion? Writing steamy, romantic stories that leave his readers panting. He's currently focusing on ABDL MM romances, but his collection is diverse and there are books for everyone's tastes. If you're looking for straight to gay, first time, BBC, sissification, and more, you're going to find them on his author page.

He lives to pamper his readers, every kiss means a lot more than what meets the eye, and he loves his Alpha males. Making sure that every gay first time feels different, Michael Levi writes his stories with a cup of coffee by his side. And for inspiration, he always opens up a photo of his new crush.

9 798777 289728